The Lemonade War

by David E. Page

illustrated by Mel Crawford

Willowisp Press®

For Eric, Maryanne, Kelley, Brant, Andrea, Jack, and, of course, Galway

Published by Willowisp Press, Inc.
801 94th Avenue North, St. Petersburg, Florida 33702

Printed in the United States of America

2 4 6 8 10 9 7 5 3 1

ISBN 0-87406-648-4

CONTENTS

1
Too Hot to Walk

The best thing about summer is that there is no school. That means you can stay home all day and play with the Hip-No-Tize Big-Screen, 16-Bit, Color-Graphics, Stereo-Sound Game System.

That's just what Julie and I do.

Julie is my best friend—most of the time. Sometimes she's my best enemy. Usually it's nothing serious. Usually Julie is just being a pain.

But one thing Julie and I almost never fight about is video games. We are the

best players in the whole world. We should be. We own just about every video game Hip-No-Tize makes.

Sometimes the games cost a lot. When they do, we put our money together and split the cost of the game. Then we take turns playing it.

My sister, Christi, says that we are wasting our time. I think she says that because she's not very good at playing video games.

"Pam," said Christi to me one

morning, "are you and Julie going to play that stupid game all day again?"

"Yes, and it's *not* a stupid game," I said. "Julie and I have gotten to the twelfth dungeon of Naughty Ninja's Revenge."

"It *is* a stupid game," Christi argued. "You should go outside and get some fresh air. Come to the walk-a-thon with me."

"It's *not* a stupid game," I repeated. "What walk-a-thon are you talking about?"

"Today is the day of the neighborhood walk-a-thon," said Christi. "I told you about it weeks ago. You were too busy playing with your dumb video games to listen to me."

"They are *NOT* dumb!" I insisted.

"They're not important like the walk-a-thon," said Christi. "People who sign up for it get their friends to donate

money for every mile they walk. Then the money goes to charity," she explained.

"Oh, yeah," I said. It was hard to argue with Christi sometimes. "Well, maybe I'll just donate something. And anyway—it's too hot outside for a walk-a-thon."

"You don't have to do any walking," said Christi. "You could help out at one of the watering stations."

"What's a watering station?" I asked.

"That's where the people walking can stop to get a quick snack or something cold to drink. There is going to be a watering station only a couple of blocks away from here."

Just then, there was a knock at the door downstairs. I heard Julie yell my name. She sounded excited.

"Come on in!" I called out.

Julie burst into my room a second later. She was out of breath.

"Prince Vince is here!" she shouted.

2
Video Idiots

"Really?" I asked in an excited voice.

"Really!" squealed Julie.

"Yahoo!" we both screamed.

"What are you talking about?" Christi asked. She had to shout to be heard. "Who is Prince Vince?"

"It's not a 'who,'" I said. "It's a 'what.'"

"It's the newest game for the Hip-No-Tize game system," Julie explained. "We've been waiting forever for it to come out. It just now got to the stores."

We both screamed again.

"Oh, brother," said Christi. "I'm leaving for the walk-a-thon. Just make sure you two vidiots are here when Mom calls."

"What's a 'vidiot'?" I asked as we followed her downstairs.

"A vidiot," said Christi, "is a video idiot." The door slammed behind her as she walked out.

I was glad she was gone. It's hard to talk about video games in front of people who really don't know anything about them.

"The ad for the game was in this

morning's paper," Julie said. We ran and got the ad section of the newspaper.

There it was, Prince Vince! It wasn't only the latest of all the video games. I just knew it had to be the greatest, too.

"It sure costs a lot," I said.

"Yeah," Julie agreed. "I don't know if I have enough money for my half."

"I know I don't have enough for my half," I said. My piggy bank was empty.

"Maybe we can get our allowances early," Julie suggested.

"My mom says I've been getting my allowance early for so long that she really doesn't owe me another one until my twenty-first birthday," I said.

We decided to have a snack. Food helps people think better.

"Maybe we can get jobs," said Julie.

"We're too young," I said, shaking my head.

"There are jobs we can do," said Julie. "We could walk people's dogs for them."

"It's too hot outside," I said. "We'd end up walking hot dogs." We both laughed.

"We could start a maid service," suggested Julie. "You know, we could sweep and dust and do dishes for people."

"Are you kidding?" I said. "I spend a lot of time getting out of helping my mother do housework. I don't want to do it for someone else."

"I've got it!" cried Julie. "I have the perfect idea for what we can do to make some money!"

3
A Great Idea

I waited almost a minute. Then I asked, "What's your idea?" Julie always makes me ask.

"We can make a lemonade stand," she said. "My mother told me all about them once. When she was a kid, she and her friends would sell lemonade from a stand in their front yard."

"Hey, that's not a bad idea," I said. "It's so hot outside, I bet we could make a million dollars." I pictured people lining up for miles to buy a cold glass of lemonade.

Then I had another thought. "We don't have any money to buy lemonade mix," I said. We were back where we started.

"We've got lots of lemonade mix at our house," said Julie.

"Great," I said. "And at my house we have a big five-gallon cooler-type of jug we can use to keep it cold."

We both ran off to get what we needed.

I lugged the jug from the garage and rinsed it out. I found a card table we could use for the stand. I also got a piece of poster board and started to make a sign. It was almost finished by the time Julie came back.

"Here's the lemonade mix," she said. She held up three packages. "This should get us started." She looked at the sign. "What's that?"

"It's our sign," I said. I held it up for her to see.

"Hey," said Julie, "why does your name go first?"

"Because I made the sign," I said. I started to draw some flowers on it.

"But the lemonade stand was *my* idea," said Julie.

"Well, we're using *my* jug," I said. "And we'll be setting up the stand in *my* yard."

"Well, we're using *my* lemonade," said Julie. "And we can set up the stand in *my* yard." She crossed her arms in that stubborn way she does. Julie is often very stubborn.

"It's not *your* lemonade," I said. "It's your mother's." Julie could be such a baby!

"Well, it's not *your* jug or *your* card table or *your* yard," said Julie. "They belong to your parents!"

I was pretty mad by this time.

"If that's the way you feel," I said, "then you can do it on your own!"

Pam and Julie's
ICE-COLD
LEMONADE
25¢

"Fine!" Julie snapped. "I'll just take my lemonade mix and go!"

"Fine," I said.

"Fine!" she snapped again, and she stomped back to her home. I watched her go. I watched the lemonade mix go with her.

4
Now What?

Now she had done it! Julie could be so stubborn. How was I going to get the money to buy Prince Vince? I wondered if I could borrow it from Christi. No, my sister would never go for that. Maybe I could blackmail her.

I was thinking about that when the phone rang. I knew it would be my mother. She called every day from work to make sure everything was all right. I don't know why. Everything was always all right, except for the time Julie had called and I forgot about the water

running in the bathtub. So I made a little mistake!

I answered the phone.

“Hello, dear. How are you doing?” I was right. It was my mother.

“I’m doing terrible,” I said. “Julie and I had a fight. We’re best enemies.”

“Again?” said Mom. “Can’t you two go for a week without arguing?”

“It was her fault,” I said. “She’s too stubborn.”

"It seems to me that you can be a little stubborn yourself," Mom pointed out. "What's the problem this time?"

I explained about Prince Vince and the lemonade.

"Why couldn't you just put Julie's name first?" asked Mom.

"Mom," I said, "you're supposed to be on my side!"

"Excuse me, Your Highness!" said Mom. "If you two can't play together, then play separately. Why don't you build your own lemonade stand?"

"How can I do that?" I asked. "We don't have any lemonade mix."

"We have a lemon tree in the backyard," said Mom.

"So?" I asked.

"Pam," said Mom, "you can be so trying sometimes. Lemonade is made from lemons, sugar, and water."

"Really?" I said. "That's pretty neat. I thought lemonade only came in a package."

"Oh, Pamela," said my mother. She always called me that just before she got one of her headaches. "I have to go. Just a little bit of work and you'll have some great lemonade. Good luck, and don't make a mess."

I promised her I wouldn't. Then we hung up.

All right! Things were looking better!

5
This Means War!

Mom had said it would just be "a little bit of work." I don't know who she thought she was kidding!

I went out to the backyard to pick some lemons. Most of them were out of reach so I had to climb the tree. Those trees have thorns! I was poked so many times I thought I was a pin cushion!

Picking the lemons turned out to be the easy part.

Next, I had to wash the lemons. Then, I had to cut them in half. After that, I had to squeeze them by hand. It was hard work!

Plus, not only the juice came out, but also the seeds and bits of pulp. I used a spoon to get the seeds out. Well, most of the seeds.

I filled the jug with ice, water, and the lemon juice. My mother had said all I needed now was sugar. What she hadn't told me was that we were almost out of sugar. There was only about half a cup left in the box. I stirred it into the lemonade.

It looked pretty good. Then I tasted it. *Ohhh!* It was sour, and not just a little sour. It was *very* sour.

Oh well. It was all I had, so it had to do.

I set up the card table at the end of the driveway and covered it with an old tablecloth. I put up my sign—after I crossed out Julie's name. (I didn't want her getting any of the credit.) Then I lugged the jug and some paper cups out to my stand and waited.

What happened next was not what I was waiting for.

Julie came out of her house dragging an old wooden crate. She set it up in her front yard and went back inside.

What was she up to?

When she came out again, she put up a sign that read:

She gave me a look, then went back inside her house again.

How dare she try to sell lemonade without me! I marched right across the street when I saw her coming back out. This time she was carrying a big glass pitcher of lemonade and ice.

"What do you think you're doing?" I asked.

"I'm making my own lemonade stand," said Julie as nastily as she could.

"You can't do that," I said. "I was here first!"

"It was my idea first," said Julie.

I wasn't going to get into that again.

"Well, we'll just see who sells the most lemonade," I said. I marched back across the street to my stand.

If it's a war she wants, I thought, *it's a war she's going to get!*

6
When in Doubt, Shout!

I was so mad I could spit.

Julie was selling lemonade right across the street from me. People might go to her stand instead of mine. If they did that, I might not make enough money to buy Prince Vince. That would be horrible! I had to find a way to sell more lemonade than Julie. But how?

Before I could think of anything, Julie surprised me.

"Lemonade for sale!" she called out loudly. "Come and get your lemonade!"

That rat! With her shouting like that, everyone would go to her stand instead of mine. She was advertising!

I couldn't let her get away with that.

"Ice-cold lemonade!" I called out. "Get your ice-cold lemonade!" I made sure to yell a little more loudly than Julie had.

"Julie's party-time lemonade!" yelled Julie. "Only 25 cents a glass." She was trying to out-shout me.

"Come and get it!" I screamed. "Nice, refreshing lemonade!"

"A party in every glass!" shrieked Julie. "Try my lemonade!" She was turning red in the face.

"Come and buy my lemonade or else!" I screeched at the top of my lungs. My throat was beginning to hurt.

"What is going on out there!"

Both Julie and I looked around. Mrs. Muffle, from next door, had her head out of her window.

"Be quiet, both of you!" Mrs. Muffle said angrily. "I'm trying to put my baby down for his nap!"

"Mrs. Muffle," said Julie and I almost at the same time, "would you like to buy some lemonade?"

"No!" she snapped. "I want you to be quiet!" She pulled her head back inside and slammed the window with a BANG!

A moment later, we heard a baby crying.

I looked at Julie and she looked at me. I almost began to giggle. For a moment, I thought Julie was going to start laughing, too. Then I remembered that Julie and I were best enemies right now.

Suddenly, Julie stuck her tongue out at me. That did it! I promised myself I would sell more lemonade than Julie.

I even had a plan.

7

Of All the Dirty Tricks!

I should have thought of it sooner. I had the perfect plan to sell more lemonade than Julie.

I went back into the house and got my markers. When I came out, I crossed out the 25-cent price on my sign. Then, I changed it to 20 cents. When people saw that my lemonade was cheaper than Julie's, they would buy from me.

When Julie saw my sign, she looked like she would explode. She took her sign down and marched back into her house.

I had won! She was quitting!

But I was wrong. She was coming back out again.

Julie had changed her sign, too. Now her lemonade was 15 cents.

Of all the dirty tricks! I couldn't let her get the better of me. I lowered my price to 10 cents.

I thought Julie was going to have a fit. She stamped the ground and made all

kinds of faces. Then she changed her price to five cents a glass.

What was I going to do? If I dropped my price any lower I would be giving my lemonade away.

Then I had another great idea. I took down my sign and went into the house. In my room I made a whole new sign:

That should do it. People like to buy things that are all-natural. I went back out to my stand.

When I got outside, I was surprised. Julie had also made a new sign:

This was the dirtiest trick of all! She must have had a package of pink lemonade mix tucked away all along. Now her lemonade was prettier than mine! I had only one chance left.

I went into the kitchen and got the only bag we had left of my favorite chocolate chip cookies. Then I made a little sign to put up next to my big one:

But Julie wasn't finished. She stomped right back into her house and made another sign, too. Her new sign read:

I had to think of something else. But before I could, something happened.

Julie and I saw a man coming our way. Our first customer. And he was on my side of the street!

8

First Sale of the Day

I looked at Julie with a big smile on my face.

Hah! I thought. *Now we'll see who sells the most lemonade.*

Julie glared back at me with a look that was as sour as my lemonade.

My lemonade! Oh, no! It *was* pretty sour. I hoped the man wouldn't notice.

"Hello, little lady," said the man. He wiped the sweat off his face with a hankie. "Today sure is a scorcher. I'll take a glass of that homemade lemonade of yours." He dropped a quarter on the top

of the stand.

I was too nervous to say anything. I just poured him a glass of lemonade. I made sure there was plenty of ice in it.

"Cheers," he said. He started to drink the lemonade. I held my breath.

After just two swallows, the man stopped drinking. His eyes got very big. Then they tightened into squints. When he slowly lowered the glass from his

mouth, his lips were puckered.

"Well," he said finally, "that sure is interesting lemonade." He spit out a seed. "I don't think I'll try any of those cookies, thank you."

"But mister," I said, "the cookies aren't homemade."

It was too late. He was walking across the street toward Julie's stand. Julie was smiling at me.

"Lemonade, mister?" she asked. She was talking very loudly so I would be sure to hear. She was trying to rub it in. "It's the best-tasting lemonade on the whole

street."

"It would have to be," said the man.

He dug in his pocket for a quarter while Julie poured lemonade into a glass. She handed the glass to him and watched as he took a sip.

"Ugh!" said the man. He made a face. "This lemonade is warm. Don't you have any ice?"

"Gee, mister," said Julie, "it melted a

long time ago. It's hot out here, you know."

The man shook his head and started to leave. Then he stopped and turned back to us. He had a puzzled look on his face.

"You know," he said, "this is a short block for two lemonade stands. Between the two of you there is almost a good glass of lemonade." He continued on his way.

Julie and I just stared at each other.

9

Pam and Julie to the Rescue

I don't know why, but I began to giggle. Julie saw me and started to get mad. Then, she started to giggle, too. Soon we were both laughing as hard as we could.

Before I knew it, I had walked across the street to Julie.

"I guess that man was right," Julie said. "Between us we do have a good glass of lemonade."

"Yeah," I said. I looked down and kicked a stone lying on the sidewalk. "Friends?" I asked.

"Well... sure!" said Julie.

We both smiled. We never stayed best enemies for long.

"High five!" I said. We both jumped into the air and slapped each other's hand above our heads.

"Go low!" said Julie. We knelt down and slapped hands again.

"Around the corner!" I said. I put my hand behind my back and Julie reached around and slapped it.

Then we gave each other our secret sign. (I can't tell you what it is, because then it wouldn't be a secret.)

"Well, now what are we going to do?" asked Julie. "We still don't have any money for Prince Vince."

"I don't know," I said. "Let's just forget about it for a while. Maybe a walk down to the watering station will give us an idea."

"The what?" asked Julie.

I explained about the walk-a-thon as we strolled downtown. When we got to the watering station, we could tell something was wrong. Everyone was just standing around looking hot and sweaty. My sister was mopping her face with a towel.

"What's wrong?" I asked.

"The woman who was supposed to bring the drinks hasn't shown up yet," said Christi. "It's very hot out and everyone is very thirsty."

I looked at Julie. Julie looked at me. I could tell we were both thinking the same thing. Off we ran for home.

It didn't take long for us to put Julie's lemonade into my jug with lots of ice. We lugged it back to the watering station in Julie's wagon.

Boy, was everyone glad to see us! Everyone wanted to buy some ice-cold lemonade. We even lowered the price to ten cents to make sure that everyone could afford it. By the end of the day, we must have had a million dimes.

Back at the house, we started to count the money.

"Oh, no!" said Julie when we finished. "We're 50 cents short!"

10
No More War—Today

It was true! We had the Hip-No-Tize Big-Screen, 16-Bit, Color-Graphics, Stereo-Sound Game System. But we were 50 cents away from being able to buy the new Prince Vince game.

Then I thought of something.

"Julie," I said excitedly, "let's check our pockets!" We both dug into our pockets. Each of us pulled out a quarter. It was the money from the man who had first bought our lemonade!

We were saved!

Off we went to the toy store to buy Prince Vince. On the way home, we were all smiles. "This is great," said Julie. She hugged the box.

"I'll let you know," I said. "I get to play it first."

"How do you figure?" asked Julie. She was starting to get angry.

"I was the one who gave the sales person the money," I said. "So really, *I* was the one who bought it."

"Well, I was the one who carried the money to the store," said Julie, "so really, *I* bought it."

We stood there facing each other, as mad as could be. Then we both started laughing.

We had already been best enemies once today. Once a day is enough.

About the Author

David Page lives in St. Petersburg, Florida with his dog Boris, a German shepherd/basset hound mix. He served in the United States Air Force and was stationed in England. He now works in a bookstore, but writing will always be his favorite job.

"When I was young," says David, "I wanted to be an architect. I spent a lot of time at the beach making sand castles. As a writer, I can do more than design buildings—I can make whole new worlds."